Bedtime Stories for 5 year olds

Helen Paiba was one of the most committed, knowledgeable and acclaimed children's booksellers in Britain. For more than twenty years she owned and ran the Children's Bookshop in Muswell Hill, London, which under her guidance gained a superb reputation for its range of children's books and for the advice available to its customers.

Helen was also involved with the Booksellers Association for many years and served on both its Children's Bookselling Group and the Trade Practices Committee.

In 1995 she was given honorary life membership of the Booksellers Association of Great Britain and Ireland in recognition of her outstanding services to the association and to the book trade. In the same year the Children's Book Circle (sponsored by Books for Children) honoured her with the Eleanor Farjeon Award, given for distinguished service to the world of children's books.

Books in this series

Animal Stories for 5 Year Olds

Animal Stories for 6 Year Olds

Bedtime Stories for 5 Year Olds

Bedtime Stories for 6 Year Olds

Funny Stories for 5 Year Olds

Funny Stories for 6 Year Olds

Funny Stories for 7 Year Olds

Funny Stories for 8 Year Olds

Magical Stories for 5 Year Olds

Magical Stories for 6 Year Olds

Scary Stories for 7 Year Olds

Bedtime Stories

for 5 year olds

Chosen by Helen Paiba

Illustrated by Leonie Shearing

MACMILLAN CHILDREN'S BOOKS

For Max with love HP

First published 2001 by Macmillan Children's Books

This edition published 2017 by Macmillan Children's Books
an imprint of Pan Macmillan
20 New Wharf Road, London N1 9RR
Associated companies throughout the world
www.panmacmillan.com

ISBN 978-1-5098-3886-8

1 3 5 7 9 8 6 4 2

A CIP catalogue record for this book is available from
the British Library.

Typeset by SX Composing DTP, Rayleigh, Essex
Printed and bound by CPI Group (UK) Ltd, Croydon CR0 4YY

Contents

Wonderful Worms   1
BERLIE DOHERTY

The Little Girl's Medicine   15
MARGARET WISE BROWN

The Tale of Mrs Puffin's Prize Pumpkin   29
ANNETTE ELIZABETH CLARK

The Rare Spotted Birthday Party   55
MARGARET MAHY

Lazy Jack   66
ANDREW MATTHEWS

My Naughty Little Sister and the
Big Girl's Bed   74
DOROTHY EDWARDS

A Hat for Rhinoceros 86
ANITA HEWITT

The Naughty Shoes 104
PAUL BIEGEL

Baldilocks and the Six Bears 114
DICK KING-SMITH

The Wonderful Cake-Horse 129
TERRY JONES

How the Wild Turkey Got Its Spots 136
ANNIE GATTI

Poppy and the Pigeon 143
GERALDINE KAYE

Lucy's Wish 156
ADÈLE GERAS

Teddy Robinson Goes to the
Dolls' Hospital 168
JOAN G. ROBINSON

Wonderful Worms

Berlie Doherty

The day before yesterday, Tilly Mint and Mrs Hardcastle went down to the park to find some magic. They didn't say they were going to find some magic, but that's what Tilly thought. She felt it in her bones. The birds were singing brightly in the trees, and fetching and carrying things for their nests.

But all Mrs Hardcastle seemed

1

to be interested in was worms.

"Just look at that worm, Tilly!" she said, when they walked past a bed of earth that had just been turned. "Just look at that blobby old worm!" Tilly didn't like worms.

"Eugh!" she said. "I'm not going near a worm."

Mrs Hardcastle was surprised. "I thought everyone liked worms, Tilly Mint," she said. "Worms are wonderful."

"How they wibble, and they wobble,
And they wubble all around,
How they dibble, and they dabble,
And they double up and down.

2

*How they're pink, and how they're
 poky,
How they pull across the ground,
How they wind, and how they
 wander,
How they wiggle round and round!"*

"Not to me, they're not," said
Tilly. "That worm's got nowhere to
go. He looks bored. He's like a
piece of string without a parcel."

"He's like a shoelace looking for
a shoe," laughed Mrs Hardcastle.

"He's like a piece of spaghetti
that nobody wants to eat," said
Tilly Mint.

"Don't you be so sure about
that!" Mrs Hardcastle said.

"Somebody wants to eat him.
Look!"

Just above them, on the branch
of a high tree, sat a little brown
bird, singing his head off. His eyes
were as bright as buttons. He was
watching the worm. Suddenly he
flew down from the branch, and he
hopped across to where the worm
was wriggling about with nowhere
to go, looking bored.

"Look out! Look out!" shouted
Mrs Hardcastle to the worm. But
she was too late. The hoppity bird
had put his beak right round the
worm. The worm tried to wiggle
back down into the earth. The
brown bird dug his feet in, and

4

pulled and pulled and pulled. The pink worm stretched and stretched and stretched.

And suddenly, POP! out came the worm. The brown bird fell over; then he stood up, shook his feathers, and flew off with the worm waving helplessly in his beak.

"Hooray!" Mrs Hardcastle clapped her hands.

Now it was Tilly who was surprised. "I thought you liked worms, Mrs Hardcastle," she said.

"So I do," Mrs Hardcastle said. "But I like birds more. Just think of those little baby birds, all snug and warm in their nest, waiting for their tea. They'll be very pleased when they see that worm."

"I wouldn't mind being a baby bird, all snug and warm in a nest," thought Tilly. "But I'd jump right out of it if anyone gave me worms for my tea. Fancy eating a worm!"

"I nearly ate a worm once, Tilly Mint, when I was a little girl. But oh, that was so long ago. That was years and years and years ago. I've nearly forgotten all about it."

And when Mrs Hardcastle said that, it was in her drowsy, faraway, remembery sort of voice, and her eyes seemed to be looking into long, long ago. Then she sat down on a park bench, closed them, and she fell asleep and snored.

"Crumbs!" said Tilly. "I'm in for it now! Magic-time!"

She closed her eyes, and when she opened them, she was in a dark, dark place. She seemed to be in a tiny, little, dark room, with hard, smooth, warm walls, and it was round.

"No, it isn't!" said Tilly, after a bit. "It's not round! It's egg-shaped. I must be . . . inside an . . . egg!"

She pushed her head up against the top of her egg, and the shell began to crack. She pushed her arms out against the sides of her egg, and the shell began to crunch.

She pushed her feet out through the bottom of her egg, and the shell began to crack, crunch, crumble!

And she was out into the air, into the sunshine, into the lovely blue light that was full of the song of birds.

Tilly took a deep breath and looked round her. Three fluffy birds were standing next to her, blinking in the sunlight. They were all standing on bits of shell. And underneath the bits of shell, there was straw, and grass, and twigs, and leaves, all plaited together like a warm, snug hat. They were in a nest!

8

Tilly hopped to the side of it and looked down. The nest seemed to be right at the top of the highest tree in the world. The branches began to sway in the wind.

"I'm hungry!" cheeped all the baby birds. "Very hungry."

"So am I!" thought Tilly. "Very, very hungry."

Just then, the brown bird hopped on to the side of the nest. Tilly recognised him by his eyes that were as bright as buttons, and by his dirty feet, and by the pink worm that was wriggling about in his beak. The baby birds pushed each other over in excitement.

Tilly Mint remembered what

9

Mrs Hardcastle had told her about
the wonderful worms:

"How they wibble, and they wobble,
And they wubble all around,
How they dibble, and they dabble,
And they double up and down.
How they're pink, and how they're
*   poky,*

10

How they prowl across the ground,
How they wind, and how they
wander,
How they wiggle round and
round."

The brown bird saw that Tilly had her mouth open, and he hopped over to her, and started to lower the worm into her beak!

"Oh no!" said Tilly. "I'm not that hungry! I'm not having worms for my tea!"

She took the poor old worm very gently into her beak, and climbed up on to the side of the nest. She looked down from the top of the highest tree in the world.

*"Bird in a nest on a branch in a
     tree,
Sail in the wind like a ship on the
     sea.
Worm in the beak of the bird in the
     skies,
Point to the ground, and close your
     eyes!"*

Tilly Mint spread out her fluffy,
feathery arms, and she closed her
eyes that were as bright as
buttons, and she jumped. She
floated down, and down, and down.
     And when she opened her eyes
again, she was standing on the
soft, brown earth with the little,
pink worm in her hand. She knelt

12

down and put him on the earth.

"In you go, little worm," she whispered. "You pop down there, and don't come out again till night-time."

The worm tucked his head into the soil and slithered out of sight.

Suddenly, Tilly remembered Mrs Hardcastle, fast asleep and snoring in the sunshine. She shook her arms to make quite sure there were no feathers left on, and then she woke up Mrs Hardcastle.

"Wake up, Mrs Hardcastle!" she said. "I'm ever so hungry."

Mrs Hardcastle opened her eyes. She looked at the blue sky, that was full of birdsong. She looked

up at the branches of the tallest
tree in the world, and saw, at the
very top, a little nest, swaying in
the wind like a boat on the sea.
She looked at the brown birds,
busy with their fetching and
carrying.

"Hello, Tilly Mint!" she said.
And then she said, "Let's go home,
shall we, and have our tea."

And they did.

The Little Girl's Medicine

Margaret Wise Brown

Once upon a time there was a little girl who lived out in the country on a big tobacco farm. She had no one to play with, this poor little girl, and she had to play all by herself. She played all by herself year after year and talked to her parents when they ate their meals.

One day, the little girl became sick. No one knew what was the matter. It was in late August, when they hitched up the four black mules and hauled the tobacco plants away to the big drying barns. But the little girl didn't want to go with them and drive the four big mules. She just sat.

That night there was peach ice cream for dinner, but the little girl didn't want any. She just sat. When it was time to go to bed, she didn't even care.

"Oh dear," said her mother to her father, "our little girl is sick. She loves to drive the four black mules, and yet she wouldn't go with them. She just sat. And she loves peach ice cream, but she wouldn't eat it

16

tonight. She just sat. And she didn't want to stay up and play when it was time to go to bed. Our little girl must be sick."

So they took the little girl to the doctor in the city.

The little girl's mother said to the doctor in the big city, "Doctor, my little girl is very sick."

"What is the matter with your little girl?" asked the doctor. "Has she a sore throat?"

And the little girl's mother said, "Doctor, my little girl doesn't want to drive the mules any more, and she doesn't like peach ice cream any more, and she doesn't care whether it is bedtime or not. So

17

I fear that she must be a very sick little girl."

"What!" said the doctor, "doesn't like peach ice cream! This is serious! Little girl, stick out your tongue."

So the little girl stuck out her tongue, and the doctor looked at it very carefully. "It is a perfectly good tongue that you have in your head, little girl," said the doctor. "Let me see your throat, little girl. Say Ahhhhhhhh."

So the little girl leaned her head way back, way back, and opened her mouth so wide that she looked like a baby robin asking for food. The doctor took a flashlight and peered down into the little girl's throat. "Say Ahhhhhhhh," he said.

Then he said, "Little girl, let me feel your pulse." So he held the little girl's wrist in his hand, and with his fingers he listened very carefully.

"It's a perfectly good heart that

you have in you, little girl; but if
you don't like to play any more and
don't like peach ice cream any
more, you are very sick. It would
be a pity if your brothers and
sisters caught what is wrong with
you."

"But I have no brothers and
sisters," said the little girl.

"But your cousins and friends
might catch it," said the doctor.

"Only I haven't any cousins; and
I haven't any friends," said the
little girl.

"Then the small animals in the
place might catch it," said the
doctor.

"There aren't even any small

animals," said the little girl. "Not
even a little pig. Just four big old
black mules that kick every time
anyone goes near them."

"Well," said the doctor, "this is
serious. I will have to prescribe
something to make you well."

The doctor sat there for a long
time nodding his head. Then at
last he said,

"Little girl, I have just the thing
that will make you well." So he
took out his pencil and wrote it
down on a piece of paper, folded it,
and handed it to the little girl's
mother.

The little girl's mother thanked
the doctor, and went out of his

21

office with the little girl.

"We will go right to the drug store first thing," said the little girl's mother, "and have this prescription filled before lunch." So they went into the drug store next door, and the little girl's mother handed the prescription to the druggist, still folded up as the doctor had given it to her.

The druggist was an old man, and he unfolded it slowly.

"Hmmmp," he said. Then he said it again. "Hmmmmp! Do you expect me to fill this prescription?"

"Why, of course," said the little girl's mother. "Haven't you got that kind of medicine?"

Then the druggist, old as he was, just threw back his head and hollered with laughter. "Do you know what this prescription says?" he asked.

The little girl's mother took the prescription and read it. And this is what the prescription said—

One fat puppy dog
to be given to
the little girl
immediately.
Signed
Dr Wwwww.

"I have filled prescriptions for thirty years," said the druggist,

23

"but never a prescription for a puppy dog. But wait!" he said. "Wait a minute. I think I can fill this prescription after all. Right across the street. Will you come with me?" he said.

So the little girl and her mother followed the druggist, still chortling and laughing to himself, out of the door and across the street to a house that had a back yard. And there in a box was one furry little puppy dog all by himself.

"This is the last one left," said the druggist. "They belong to my sister, and she is giving them away. So if the doctor says the little girl needs a puppy, this is how we can fill the prescription."

"My puppy?" asked the little girl. "All mine?"

"Yes," said the druggist. "That is your puppy, and you can take him right home with you this minute."

The little puppy wiggled and jumped around the little girl as if he was just as glad as she was that they would have each other to play with. He had been sitting all by himself for two long days. He hadn't even drunk the milk that was still in his saucer.

So the little girl took her puppy right home with her. They got back just as the big wagon with

the four black mules was going out
of the gate. The little girl's father
was driving.

"Hey, little girl," he called, "do
you want to go out after the last
load with me?"

"Indeed I do!" said the little girl.
"And look what I am going to
bring with me!"

She jumped out of the car with
the puppy under her arm and
climbed up on the wagon beside
her father.

"For goodness sakes!" he said.
"What in the world have you got
there?"

"This," said the little girl, "is
my medicine, and I feel much

26

better already."

"Well, come here, Medicine," said the little girl's father. "Are you going to learn to be a good tobacco farmer like me and the little girl?"

Little fat Medicine (for that was the puppy's name from then on) wiggled right up in her father's arms and licked him on the nose, and they all drove along on the wagon together behind the four black mules. Then they went home to supper.

And what do you think they had for dessert, and the fat little puppy had a spoonful of it too? Peach ice cream.

And when it was time to go to bed, up the steps scampered the little girl, and up the steps scampered the little puppy. And together that night the little girl and her Medicine went right off to sleep, all curled up in their warm little beds in the same room.

The Tale of Mrs Puffin's Prize Pumpkin

Annette Elizabeth Clark

Mrs Puffin stood on her doorstep one fine morning early in June, and looked at her garden and said, "Oh Dear! Oh dear! Dearie, dearie me."

You could not really say there was much garden to look at. There had been no rain for weeks and everything was dried up. The rose that climbed over the house was covering the ground with white petals like snow; the honeysuckle was drooping, and the tall foxgloves by the door hung their heads. Even the pinks in the near border looked shrivelled, and Mrs Puffin's neat rows of young cabbage and potatoes and peas were thirsty and dry.

"I'll go down the hill," said Mrs Puffin, "and get a bucket or two of water and give the peas a soaking before the sun gets hot."

Mrs Puffin lived in a little white cottage halfway up a hill. If you went down a lane between tall green hedges you came to another

little white house at the bottom of
the hill where her nearest
neighbour lived. His name was
Peter Pinch. Peter had a garden
too, but in spite of the hot dry
weather it was still fresh and
green. A tiny spring of clear,
bright water came out of the
hillside just by Peter's gate. It
made a little pool and then ran on,
right through his garden, past his
old apple trees and away through
fields till, I suppose, it came to a
river and went down with it to
the sea.

So Peter had all the water he
needed for his garden. His roses
were pink and white and covered

with buds; his flowers stood up straight and strong, his cabbages and potatoes and peas looked fresh and green. You would not think Peter had anything to grumble about. But he had. He grumbled every day and every time when Mrs Puffin came to fetch water from his little pool.

"Don't take too much, Mrs Puffin," he would say, "you'll empty the pool and leave none for me. Two buckets full in the morning and two in the evening is a-plenty," said Peter.

He knew quite well that the little spring went on running, and that however much water Mrs Puffin

took, the pool would soon fill
again. But Peter Pinch always
wanted to keep everything for
himself. Even the birds made him
angry. He threw stones at them to
drive them away from his garden in
summer, and he never gave them
even a crumb in winter.

On the morning that I am telling
you about, Mrs Puffin hoped that
Peter Pinch would still be asleep.
She went quietly down the hill
with her buckets. It was not really
very far, though it seemed a long
way when you came uphill with a
heavy bucket in each hand. She
looked up at Peter's window and
saw that it was shut and the

curtains were drawn. So she did not hurry. She dipped the water out of the little pool, slowly and comfortably with her big tin mug, till the pails were nearly full. Then she carried them up and watered her thirsty peas and went down again to get water for the house.

She had filled one bucket and was stooping over the second when somebody laughed and something fell with a loud splash into her pail.

Mrs Puffin jumped, and said, "Bless me!" and looked round. Peter Pinch was standing near his gate, laughing to himself. He had just dropped a large toad into the full bucket. Toads do not like being dropped into water any more than you or I would, so Mrs Puffin said, "Poor thing!" and picked him out in a hurry and wrapped him in two dock-leaves and put him in her apron pocket. She was sure Peter did not mean to be kind to the

toad, so she would not leave him there.

Peter only laughed again and said, "There's a bit of company for you, Mrs Puffin. I've got no room for him in *my* garden."

And Mrs Puffin said politely in a dignified voice, "Good *morning,* Mr Pinch," and picked up her pails and went up the hill. She put the toad down in a cool corner under some ferns by the door; and she used the water from the pail he had been in for scrubbing. There was enough in the other pail to make several cups of tea, so she did not have to go down the hill again till the cool of the day was come.

When she came back with her pails in the evening, she found the toad sitting on her doorstep. He looked at her with his bright eyes, and Mrs Puffin nodded at him, "Good evening, Master Toad," she said, "I hope I see you well."

When she had finished watering her garden he was still there, and she said good night to him when she shut the door. He was among her rows of peas next morning when she watered them, and Mrs Puffin said, "Nice morning" to him. The toad never made a sound – as you know, toads are quiet creatures – but he looked fat and comfortable, and as the days went by Mrs Puffin talked to him more and more. When she came panting up the hill with her buckets, she used to tell him how hot it was and how heavy the pails were. She told him how green Peter Pinch's garden was looking, how fat his peas were and how rosy and ripe his strawberries were getting. And at last, one evening, poor Mrs Puffin sat down and burst into tears. Peter Pinch had been so cross, she was tired, and her garden looked so dried and withered. "If only I had a little spring of water of my own," said poor Mrs Puffin, "just a little tiny spring, to keep the garden green!"

She cried and cried and the toad looked at her solemnly. He was sitting in the corner of the doorstep where he always sat in the evening. Presently he crawled off the doorstep and went slowly down the garden path. He wriggled under Mrs Puffin's gate; she thought he must be going down the lane, but she was too tired and miserable to go and look. She cried a little more, because she was really fond of her toad and she was afraid he was tired of her dried-up garden, and then she went to bed.

But when she came out with her pails very early next morning, she saw the toad again. He had not gone down the hill, after all. He was crawling under the gate of a field, a little way down the lane.

"Good morning, Master Toad," said Mrs Puffin.

The toad sat in the lane and looked wisely at her, and Mrs Puffin looked over the gate. The grass in the field was short because Farmer Brown's cows fed there, and she could see very plainly that there was a big fairy-ring in the middle of the field. And from the fairy-ring to the gate there was a little ruffled pathway through the dew, as if something had crawled across the grass.

"It seems to *me*," said Mrs Puffin to herself as she went down the hill, "that my Master Toad has been talking to the Fairies!"

When she came back the toad was in the garden again, and in the evening he was on the doorstep as usual, so Mrs Puffin knew he had come back to stay.

It was not long after this that a fat, juicy green shoot came up in the corner of Mrs Puffin's garden, in a little hollow by the hedge. Mrs Puffin looked at it and wondered what it could be, and gave it all the water she could spare to encourage it to grow.

It grew very fast and presently

Mrs Puffin said, "It's a pumpkin plant. Wherever did it come from?" She looked at the toad as if he could tell her. She thought perhaps he could, if only he could talk. She had not forgotten the morning when she saw him coming away from the fairy-ring. "And maybe," she said to herself, "the Good Folks sent me a pumpkin plant to make up for the rest of my things being spoiled this year!"

Pumpkins are rather like vegetable marrows. They like plenty of water. Mrs Puffin gave her pumpkin every drop she could spare. She emptied her scrubbing-pail and her washing-bowl into the hollow. She put all her tea-leaves round the root to keep it damp. And the pumpkin grew big green leaves and long green stalks and it blossomed with large yellow flowers.

Mrs Puffin watched it grow with joy and pride. She was so proud of it that she even told Peter Pinch about it, and he used to walk up the lane to look at it and count the flowers and wonder how many pumpkins there would be. He had none of his own, and to tell the truth he was rather jealous of Mrs Puffin. So I am afraid he was really pleased to find that when all the yellow flowers had fallen, there was only one little green pumpkin left.

Mrs Puffin was very disappointed. She had hoped she was going to have half a dozen pumpkins at least. But she only said, "One is a deal better than none," and she went on watering her pumpkin plant. And the little pumpkin grew and grew and *grew*, larger and larger, rounder and rounder till it was a most enormous pumpkin! Mrs Puffin watched it grow. She went to look at it so often that her footsteps made quite a deep little pathway across her garden. Very often she found the toad sitting in the little hollow, and she thought to herself, "He's as proud of it as I am."

When September came the pumpkin was ripe. It had turned from green to pale yellow and from yellow to bright orange. The leaves and stalks dried up and withered, but the pumpkin almost filled the little hollow. It lay there like a large round golden moon. And it was heavy. Mrs Puffin moved it gently and felt sure she could not lift it. She said to Peter Pinch, "My pumpkin's ripe, Master Pinch. I shall cut it this evening for fear it should spoil. If you like to come up the hill, I'll give you half of it. There's more than I can use."

Peter Pinch was pleased. He liked having presents given to him, though he never gave any himself. So about six o'clock that evening he went up the hill and found Mrs Puffin with a knife, all ready to cut the pumpkin.

"I'll cut it in half in the garden," said Mrs Puffin, "it's too heavy to carry into the house."

She stooped down to cut it. But as the point of her knife went into the big yellow pumpkin, Mrs Puffin said, "*Oh*!" in a startled voice. "Oh!" she said. "Oh dear! It's quite hollow. There's nothing in it, Master Pinch!"

She pulled out the knife and

there was a little bubbling sound. A tiny stream of water ran out of the hole that the knife had made.

Peter Pinch looked at it angrily. "That pumpkin's *bad*," he said. And he turned round and stomped away down the hill, very cross indeed. He was really a very grumpy old man.

Poor Mrs Puffin! She was dreadfully disappointed. She went in and sat down and made herself a large cup of tea for comfort; and she did not go out into the garden again that evening. She could not bear to look at her beautiful pumpkin.

But she looked out of her

window that night before she got
into bed. She remembered she had
not said good night to the toad. It
was a clear night with a great
bright moon, and she could see
Master Toad quite plainly sitting
by the little hollow. The pumpkin
lay there, but she could see only
part of it. The hollow was almost
filled with clear water that shone
in the moonlight and the pumpkin
was nearly covered.

"It must have held a lot of water.
It's a very odd pumpkin," said Mrs
Puffin. The she called "Good
night" to the toad and she got into
bed and went to sleep.

When she came out early next

morning with her pails, the first thing she noticed was a little stream – a tiny sparkling stream of water, running from the pumpkin hollow, along the little path that her footsteps had made right across her garden.

"Bless me!" said Mrs Puffin, "where did that come from? That pumpkin gets odder and odder."

She hurried across her garden to see what could have happened. When she came to the hollow, Master Toad sat by it looking at it solemnly and importantly. Mrs Puffin looked too; she was looking for her big pumpkin. But there was no pumpkin to be seen. The little hollow was filled with clear water that stirred and rippled gently as if it bubbled up softly from beneath.

"Oh-h-h-h!" said Mrs Puffin – and she said no more for quite a long while – as she stood there looking and thinking.

Presently she stooped down and looked close; under the ripples she thought she could just see a gleam of yellow shining. "Yes," said Mrs Puffin, and she nodded her head. "Yes, that's it, there's my pumpkin. It was a fairy pumpkin, sure enough. The Good Folks sent it to me with a spring of water in it for my garden!"

She turned and curtseyed very deeply and gratefully to the toad and said, "Thank you, Master Toad, my dear." She was sure he was pleased because his eyes sparkled like little diamonds in the sunlight.

Then Mrs Puffin put her pails on the doorstep and hurried down the hill. She stopped to make a curtsey and to say, "Thank you with all my heart" in the middle of the fairy-ring; and then she ran to Peter Pinch's cottage. She knocked on the door and threw little stones at the window till Peter Pinch opened it and put out his head (with a night-cap on it), very cross indeed at being woken so early.

Mrs Puffin said, "Peter Pinch! I've got a spring of water in my garden. It's come from my big pumpkin," which surprised him so much that he came running downstairs in two minutes, all dressed, with his night-cap still on his head.

They went up the hill together; and there was no doubt about it, there really was a spring. The water bubbled up softly in the pool in the hollow and flowed through Mrs Puffin's garden and into the field and down the hill.

"I shall never have to carry pails of water up the hill again," said

Mrs Puffin. And she never did. Spring, summer, autumn and winter, the water flowed and Mrs Puffin's garden was green and blossoming every year.

She and Master Toad lived there in great happiness and contentment for many years after. And I am glad to say that even Peter Pinch grew better-tempered when Mrs Puffin no longer needed to draw water from his spring. On summer evenings he would often hobble up the hill for a chat; and they would talk together of Mrs Puffin's prize pumpkin, while Master Toad sat by them on the doorstep.

The Rare Spotted Birthday Party

Margaret Mahy

It was Mark's birthday in two days' time but he was not happy about it.

His mother had made a wonderful cake – round, brown and full of nuts and raisins and cherries. There were balloons and party hats hidden in the high cupboard with the Christmas

decorations and old picture books.
But Mark was not happy.

It was his birthday in two days'
time and he had the measles.

Everyone was getting the
measles.

"Measles are going around," said
Mark's little sister Sarah.

John with the sticking-out ears
had the measles.

The twins next door – James and
Gerald – had the measles. They
had the same brown hair, the same
brown eyes, and now they both
had the same brown spots.

Mark's friend, Mousey, had the
measles. Mousey had so many
freckles everyone was surprised

that measles could find any room on him.

"Mousey must be even more spotted than I am," said Mark.

"Mousey must be more spotted than *anyone*," Sarah said. "He is a rare spotted mouse."

"It's worse for me," said Mark. "No one can have a birthday when they are covered in spots."

"No one would be able to come," said Sarah. "Do you feel sick, Mark?"

"I feel a bit sick," said Mark. "Even if I *could* have a birthday, I don't think I would want it."

"That is the worst thing," said Sarah. "Not even *wanting* a birthday is worst of all."

Two days later, when the birthday really came, Mark did not feel sick any more. He just felt spotty.

He opened his presents at breakfast.

His mother and father had given him a camera. It was small, but it would take real pictures. Sarah gave him a paint box. (She always gave him a paint box. Whenever Mark got a new paint box, he gave Sarah the old one.)

All morning they painted.

"It feels funny today," said Mark. "It doesn't feel like a birthday. It doesn't feel special at all."

Sarah had painted a class of children. Now she began to paint spots on them.

Lunch was plain and healthy.

In the afternoon Mark's mother started to brush him all over. She brushed his hair. She brushed his dressing-gown, though it was new and did not need brushing. She brushed his slippers.

"We will have a birthday drive," she said. "The car windows will stop the measles from getting out."

They drove out into the country and up a hill that Mark knew. "There's Peter's house," he said. "Peter-up-the-hill! He has measles too."

"We might pay him a visit for a moment," Mark's mother said. "He won't catch measles from you if he has them already."

The front door was open. They rang the bell and walked in. Then Mark got a real surprise! The room was full of people. Lots of people were boys wearing dressing-gowns – all of them spotty boys, MEASLE-Y boys.

"Happy birthday! Happy birthday!" they shouted.

There was John with the sticking-out ears. His ears were still a bit spotty around the edges. There were the twins, James and Gerald. Measles made them look more like each other than ever before. There was Mousey. You could not tell where his freckles left off and his measles began. There was Peter-up-the-hill in a pink dressing-gown, and Peter-next-to-the-shop in a bluey-green one.

"Happy birthday! Happy

birthday!" they all shouted.

"It's a measle party," Mark's mother explained. "So many people are getting over measles we decided to have a measle party on your birthday."

"Have you brought my birthday cake?" asked Mark.

"It is in a tin box in the back of the car," said his mother. "I would not forget an important thing like that."

What a funny, spotty, measle-y party! All the guests except Sarah were wearing dressing-gowns.

They played a game called 'Painting Spots on an Elephant'. They played 'Measle-y Chairs' (this is like 'Musical Chairs' except that people who play it have to have the measles).

Sarah found a piece of blue chalk and drew spots all over her face. "I've got *blue* measles," she said. "Mine are very unusual spots." (She did not like being the only person without any spots at all.)

Then came the party food. They had spaghetti and meat balls. They had fruit salad and ice cream, and glasses of orange juice. The fruit salad had strawberries and grapes in it.

Then Mark's mother brought in the cake she had made. It was iced

with white icing, and it was
spotted and dotted and spattered
with pink dots.

"Measles!" cried Mark. "The
cake's got measles!" He thought it
was the funniest, nicest cake he
had ever seen. The measles made it
taste extremely delicious.

A measle cake for a measle
party! A spotty cake for a dotty
party!

"I don't think I'll have a piece of
cake," said Sarah. "I don't feel very
well . . . I feel all hot and cross."

"Heigh-ho!" said Mark's mother.
"I think I know what is wrong."

"You are probably getting the
measles," said Mark. "Perhaps *you*

will have a measle party too."

"We will think of something else for Sarah," said his mother. "But now we must go home."

"Can't I have a measle party as well?" Sarah pleaded. "I want one too."

"Measle parties are like comets," said Mark's mother. "If you see one in twenty years you are lucky."

She took Mark and Sarah home, with Mark thinking to himself that it was worth getting the measles at birthday time if a special measles party was the result.

After all, not many people have been to one.

Lazy Jack

Andrew Matthews

A bit further along Hay Way, Jack lived with his widowed mother. Jack's mother took in washing and ironing and worked hard to earn a bit of money, but Jack didn't do any work at all. He was so lazy, he wouldn't even feed himself. When they had peas, his mother would use a spoon to flick them across the room into Jack's mouth.

One Monday, Jack's mother could stand it no more. She told Jack that if he didn't start earning his keep, she'd turn him out of the house. So on Tuesday, Jack got himself a day's work at Palm Farm, and the farmer, Mr Palmer, paid him a penny. Because he'd never earned wages before, Jack didn't know what to do with the penny. He held it tightly in his hand, but it slipped out of his grip and lost itself as he was crossing a stream on his way home.

"You silly boy!" his mother told him. "You should have put it in your pocket!"

"You know best, Mother," said Jack.

On Wednesday, Jack went to work for Howard the Cowherd, who gave him a big jug of milk for his wages. Jack put the jug in his pocket, but by the time he got home all the milk had sloshed out of it and he was wetter than a fish's slippers.

"You silly boy!" said his mother. "You should have carried it home on your head!"

"I won't be so silly next time," said Jack.

Thursday came, and Jack got a job at Mary's Dairy. Mary paid him with a big slab of butter. Jack

put the butter on his head and off
he went. It was such a hot day that
by the time he reached home, the
butter had melted into his hair
and made it as greasy as the inside
of an old frying pan.

"You silly boy!" said his mother.
"You should have carried it home

in your hands!"

"I won't make that mistake again," said Jack.

On Friday, Jack worked for Mr Laker the Baker, who gave him a handsome tomcat. Jack carried the cat in his hands, but the cat wriggled so much it was like carrying a furry python. Before he'd gone very far, old Tom gave him such a bite with his sharp teeth and such a scratch with his sharp claws that Jack let him go.

"You silly boy!" said his mother. "You should have tied a rope around it and walked it home!"

"Of course I should! You're quite right," said Jack.

On Saturday, Jack went to work for Mr Mopp at the butcher's shop. Mr Mopp was so pleased with him that he gave him a string of sausages for his pay. Jack tied a rope around the sausages and walked them home. By the time he got there, the sausages were covered in so much grit and dust that they had to be thrown away.

"You silly boy!" said his mother. "You should have carried them home over your shoulders!"

"Whatever you say, Mother," said Jack.

The following Monday, Jack went to work for Mr Howman the Ploughman, and Mr Howman gave him a donkey. The donkey kicked and brayed, but at last Jack got it over his shoulders and staggered home.

On the way, Jack met a couple of strangers – a farmer and his little daughter. The daughter had been ill and since her illness she'd been as miserable as rain in a rusty tin. The farmer had taken his daughter to the best doctors in the land, and they'd all told him the only thing that would make her properly better was to have a good laugh. The farmer had heard about how silly the people of Waffam were and he was bringing her on a visit in the hope that something would make her chuckle.

Well, when she saw Jack stumbling along the road with a donkey over his shoulders, and the donkey's ears and legs waggling about in the air, the girl laughed until tears filled her eyes and she was better at once.

The farmer was overjoyed, he gave Jack a big bag of gold.

"You ride home on the donkey, lad, and keep a tight hold on that bag of money," said the farmer.

"Right you are. I'll do that," said Jack.

And he made no mistakes this time, I can tell you.

My Naughty Little Sister and the Big Girl's Bed

Dorothy Edwards

A long time ago, when my naughty little sister was a very small girl, she had a nice cot with pull-up sides so that she couldn't fall out and bump herself.

My little sister's cot was a very pretty one. It was pink, and had pictures of fairies and bunny rabbits painted on it.

It had been my old cot when I
was a very small child and I had
taken care of the pretty pictures.
I used to kiss the fairies "good
night" when I went to bed, but my
bad little sister did not kiss them
and take care of their pictures.
Oh no!

My naughty little sister did
dreadful things to those poor
fairies. She scribbled on them with
pencils and scratched them with
tin-lids, and knocked them with
poor old Rosy-Primrose, her doll,
until there were hardly any
pictures left at all. She said,
"Nasty fairies. Silly old rabbits."

There! Wasn't she a bad child?

You wouldn't do things like that, would you?

And my little sister jumped and jumped on her cot. After she had been tucked up at night-time she would get out from under the covers, and jump and jump. And when she woke up in the morning she jumped and jumped again,

until one day, when she was jumping, the bottom fell right out of the cot, and my naughty little sister, and the mattress, and the covers, and poor Rosy-Primrose all fell out on to the floor!

Then our mother said, "That child must have a bed!" Even though our father managed to mend the cot, our mother said, "She must have a bed!"

My naughty little sister said, "A big bed for me?"

And our mother said, "I am afraid so, you bad child. You are too rough now for your poor old cot."

My little sister wasn't ashamed

of being too rough for her cot. She was pleased because she was going to have the new bed, and she said, "A big girl's bed for me!"

My little sister told everybody that she was going to have a big girl's bed. She told her kind friend the window-cleaner man, and the coalman, and the milkman. She told the dustman too. She said, "You can have my old cot soon, dustman, because I am going to have a big girl's bed." And she was as pleased as pleased.

But our mother wasn't pleased at all. She was rather worried. You see, our mother was afraid that my naughty little sister would jump and jump on her new bed, and scratch it, and treat it badly. My naughty little sister had done such dreadful things to her old cot, that my mother was afraid she would spoil the new bed too.

Well now, my little sister told the lady who lived next door all about her new bed. The lady who lived next door to us was called Mrs Jones, but my little sister used to call her Mrs Cocoa Jones because she used to go in and have a cup of cocoa with her every morning.

Mrs Cocoa Jones was a very kind lady, and when she heard about the new bed she said, "I have a little yellow eiderdown and a yellow counterpane upstairs, and they are too small for any of my beds, so when your new bed comes, I will give them to you."

My little sister was excited, but when she told our mother what Mrs Cocoa had said, our mother shook her head.

"Oh dear," she said, "what will happen to the lovely eiderdown and counterpane when our bad little girl has them?"

Then, a kind aunt who lived near us said, "I have a dear little green nightie-case put away in a drawer. It belonged to me when I was a little girl. When your new bed comes you can have it to put your nighties in like a big girl."

My little sister said, "Good. Good" because of all the nice things she was going to have for her bed. But our mother was more worried than ever. She said, "Oh dear! That pretty nightie-case. You'll spoil it, I know you will!"

But my little sister went on being pleased as pleased about it.

Then one day the new bed arrived. It was a lovely shiny brown bed, new as new, with a lovely blue stripy mattress to go on it: new as new. And there was a new stripy pillow too. Just like a real big girl would have.

My little sister watched while my

mother took the poor old cot to pieces, and stood it up against the wall. She watched when the new bed was put up, and the new mattress was laid on top of it. She watched the new pillow being put into a clean white case, and when our mother made the bed with clean new sheets and clean new blankets, she said, "Really big girl! A big girl's bed – all for me."

Then Mrs Cocoa Jones came in, and she was carrying the pretty yellow eiderdown and the yellow counterpane. They were very shiny and satiny like buttercup flowers, and when our mother put them on top of the new bed, they looked beautiful.

Then our kind aunt came down the road, and *she* was carrying a little parcel, and in the little parcel was the pretty green nightie-case. My little sister ran down the road to meet her because she was so excited. She was more excited still when our aunt picked up her little nightdress and put it into the pretty green case and laid the green case on the yellow shiny eiderdown.

My little sister was so pleased that she was glad when bedtime came.

And, what do you think? She got carefully, carefully into bed with

Rosy-Primrose, and she laid herself down and stretched herself out – carefully, carefully like a good, nice girl.

And she didn't jump and jump, and she didn't scratch the shiny brown wood, or scribble with pencils or scrape with tin-lids. Not

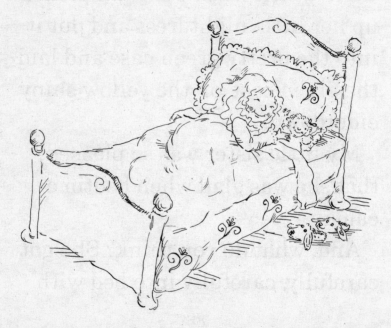

ever! Not even when she had had the new bed a long, long time.

My little sister took great care of her big girl's bed. She took great care of her shiny yellow eiderdown and counterpane and her pretty green nightie-case.

And whatever do you think she said to me?

She said, "You had the fairy pink cot before I did. But this is my very own big girl's bed, and I am going to take great care of my very own bed, like a big girl!"

A Hat for Rhinoceros

Anita Hewitt

Rhinoceros found an old straw hat, which he wore on his head to keep off the sun.

It fitted him perfectly.

It kept his head cool.

He did not know what he would do without it.

While he was dozing one day, with his hat on, Monkey came along and stole it. By the time Rhinoceros came to his senses,

Monkey was high in a mango tree with the hat pulled well down over his ears.

Rhinoceros came to the tree and said, "You'll excuse me mentioning it, but it's *my* hat."

"You hat, my hat, whose hat?" said Monkey. "It's on *my* head, and

that's where I'll keep it."

Rhinoceros did not argue with Monkey. He was much too proud. He said to himself, "Oh well, I shall just have to manage, I suppose."

He went to the bank of the great grey river and put himself up to his ears in the mud. But the heat of the sun on his tender bare head was a burning pain. And it made him angry.

He *needed* a hat.

He was *used* to a hat.

He could not do *without* a hat.

He heaved himself out of the mud and said, "I'll have that hat. I'll have that hat if I have to climb the tree to get it. Disgraceful! That's what it is, disgraceful. A peaceful Rhinoceros finds a hat, and he can't do without it, and *then* what happens? It's stolen, with never a please or thank you. It's time that monkey was taught a lesson, before he starts stealing our tails and our horns."

Rhinoceros stumped along to the mango tree. Monkey still sat there, with the hat on his head.

Rhinoceros backed away from the tree trunk. He lowered his head and he flicked up his tail.

"Ah-oop one. Ah-oop two. Ah-oop three. And charge!" he said. And he shot at the tree like a great grey rocket. Faster and faster! Bang! He hit it.

The roots of the mango tree shook in the earth, and its branches beat about in the air. Rhinoceros stiffened his legs, and waited. When Monkey fell, he would catch him, and spank him, and then he would make him return the hat.

But the only thing that fell from the tree was a mango fruit, and Rhinoceros ate it, pretending that this was what he had come for.

"But I'll have that hat, I'll have that hat, if I have to fly in the air to get it."

He went away and found three sticks, which he tied together with strips of grass.

"A three-stick, that's what it is," he said. "A long thin three-stick, good for poking."

He waited till Monkey fell asleep, then he picked up the three-stick and went to the tree. He could see Monkey's tail and the back of the hat.

"Carefully does it," Rhinoceros said.

He wriggled the three-stick up through the branches and poked at the hat, very gently at first. Then he poked again. Then he pushed. Then he prodded.

"Bother!" he said. "Is it *stuck* to his head?"

Rhinoceros felt his temper rising. He jabbed and jerked and joggled the three-stick until he was hot and exceedingly angry.

"Off with you, hat. Come off," he snorted. "Oh bother, *now* what's happened to it?"

The three-stick had jabbed through the brim of the hat, and Rhinoceros stared at a tiny blue circle where sky could be seen through the little round hole. He dropped the three-stick and said to himself, "I *will* have that hat." And he went away.

He wandered far and wide in the

jungle, thinking and planning, and wanting his hat. But all his plans seemed silly and useless.

He stopped at last on the edge of the jungle, and there he saw a peculiar sight. Snake, who usually laid in the grass, was lying curled up in a wicker basket.

Sitting in front of the basket, cross-legged, was a small brown man who was playing a pipe.

"I like that music," Rhinoceros said. "It's whistly, weavy, sway-about music."

Out of the basket came Snake's brown head, pointing upwards towards the sky. Then his body came out of the basket too, slowly

and smoothly stretching upwards.
The small brown man began to
move, swaying his body in time to
the music. Snake swayed too,
bending *his* body; swaying to one
side, the other side, back again,
swaying and swaying in time to the
music.

"Well," said Rhinoceros. "What a
strange sight! But now I must go. I
have plans to make."

But he did *not* go. He was caught
by the music. The tune held him
fast and he could not get free of it.
Whistling and weaving and
slipping about, it seemed to get
right inside his head. Then slowly,
Rhinoceros started to sway. He felt

uncomfortable and giddy, so he tried to stop, but the tune would not let him. Then, just as he thought he would fall on the grass, the brown man took the pipe from his mouth.

The music stopped whistling and Snake stopped swaying. Rhinoceros stood quite still on the grass, but everything seemed to be spinning around him. Snake, the brown man, the sky, and the trees were all mixed up in a whirling dance. By the time he had sorted them out again, the brown man had gone, and Snake was beside him, asking anxiously, "Are you all right?"

"I think so, thank you," Rhinoceros said. "But I felt so giddy I nearly fell over." Then, seeing that Snake was still looking worried, he tried to smile and make a joke, "It's lucky I stay on the ground all the time, and don't go climbing trees," he said. "If I'd been on a branch, I *should* have gone crash."

It was then that Rhinoceros thought of Monkey, sitting at home in the mango tree.

He bent his head, and whispered to Snake.

"Yes," said Snake, "I think it would work. But can you whistle, Mr Rhinoceros?"

"Yes," said Rhinoceros. "Thrush Bird taught me."

"Are you sure you remember the tune?" asked Snake.

"I can't forget it," Rhinoceros said. "It got itself into my head and it stayed there. To tell you the truth, I'll be glad to get rid of it."

"Then come," said Snake, and he glided away. Rhinoceros followed across the jungle until they came to the mango tree.

Monkey still sat there, hat on head.

"I'm afraid there's no basket," Rhinoceros whispered. "But perhaps you can lie on that pile of leaves. I'll stand in front of you, here, like this."

Snake curled up on the pile of leaves, and Rhinoceros whistled the brown man's tune. Whistling and weaving and slipping about, the music went on and on and on. Out of the leaves rose Snake's brown head, pointing upwards towards the sky. His body came out of the leaves as well, slowly and smoothly stretching upwards. Then Snake swayed to one side, the other side, back again, swaying and swaying in time to the music.

Monkey looked down from the mango tree, and he could not take his eyes off Snake, and Rhinoceros went on whistling the tune, and

98

Snake went on swaying and swaying and swaying.

Then, very slowly, Monkey swayed too, bending his body in time to the music. He tried to stop, because he felt giddy. But he could not take his eyes off Snake, and he could not escape from the slippery music. Everything seemed to be spinning around him. Snake, Rhinoceros, trees and sky were all mixed up in a whirling dance.

It was then that he swayed and swayed and swayed until he swayed right off the mango branch. He crashed through the tree in a shower of leaves and fell on his tail in front of Rhinoceros.

"Well?" said Rhinoceros. "What do you say?"

"I'm sorry," said Monkey.

"Good," said Rhinoceros. "Now you will kindly return my hat."

Monkey tugged the hat from his head. Rhinoceros took it and stared at it happily. Then he began to mutter and frown, looking down at the little round hole that the poking three-stick had made in the brim. He had worried about the hole all day. But soon he was smiling again, and saying, "Of course, of course, how silly I am. I ought to have thought of that before. The hole in the hat is really quite useful."

He picked a hibiscus flower from a bush, and tucked it carefully into the hole.

He put on the hat and smiled to himself.

"Monkey," he said. "Run along and be good. Run along quickly."

Snake looked up at the flower-trimmed hat.

"It fits you perfectly," he said.

"Yes," said Rhinoceros. "Yes, it does. And it keeps my head cool. That's why I wear it."

He went away to the great grey river, and stood on the bank, very quiet and still.

Was he *really* fast asleep?

The air grew cool and the moon

came up, shining its silver light on the river. And in the shadowy water-mirror, between the rippling reflection of trees, the satisfied face of a big Rhinoceros smiled, beneath a flower-trimmed hat.

The Naughty Shoes

Paul Biegel

Have you ever crawled into bed at night with your shoes on? Of course not! You take them off and put them under your chair or under your bed. Grown-ups do the same thing. So just imagine how many thousands of pairs of shoes stand under beds and chairs during the long, dark night, while their owners lie under the covers asleep.

Do the shoes also sleep? Heavens no! Shoes never get tired. Listen to this:

One night my father's left shoe said to my father's right shoe, "I am sick and tired of taking Father places; all day long I have to go where he wants to go – this way and that way, up way and down way, in way and out way! Now I am going by myself, and I am going the *other* way!"

"I am going with you," said my father's right shoe.

So off they went through the open window, out into the dark street. It sounded like a man walking in the street, but it was

105

only an empty pair of shoes, going the other way.

"Coming along?" they called through the open window to the neighbours' shoes. And the shoes of the neighbours – husband and wife – joined my father's shoes; their neighbours' shoes came along too, and the shoes of the neighbours of the neighbours, all down the block.

It became quite a parade. Clickety-click went the high heels; boom-boom went the heavy boots; schwee-schwee went the rubbers. Shoes, shoes, and more shoes – old pairs, new pairs, worn-out pairs; shiny shoes, unpolished shoes, scuffed shoes; brown ones, black ones, big ones, small ones. They walked, they ran, they skipped – always the other way, for this was the Free Shoe Parade and their owners' feet were all at home under the covers.

"Left belongs to right!" called

the shoes. "Hold on to each other by the laces!"

But Grandma's left shoe lost track of Grandma's right shoe. And the shoes without laces couldn't hold on to each other at all.

"Where are you? Where are you?" voices called in the dark.

"I'm here! I'm here!" came the answers from here and there and everywhere.

But which belonged to which? There was too much confusion for the right shoes to find their lefts and for the left shoes to find their rights.

"Never mind," someone shouted.

"Every shoe for himself from now on. We don't need to be paired off."

And off they went again. Single left shoes and unattached right shoes. Hoppety-hop. The very dainty and the very shiny shoes waded through all the mud puddles, what fun!

But the old, scuffed shoes, the dirty and unkempt ones, walked primly with neat little steps and avoided the puddles. The shoes of old people hopped, skipped, and jumped. The children's shoes took slow, dignified steps. Shoes without feet cramped inside them. Shoes who were their own masters. They all had a glorious time, a wonderful marvellous time!

But the fun had to come to an end. The sun came up and shooed away the darkness.

"We have to go home! We have to get back before our people get out of bed!" shouted the shoes, and the jolly parade changed into a scramble of confusion and panic.

Most of the shoes had lost their way and did not know how to get home. As the sun rose higher in the sky, they stampeded through the streets, clickety-click, boom-boom, schwee-schwee, scuff-scuff. Boots stomped over slippers. Shoes tripped over their untied laces.

110

Toe-caps banged against toe-caps, and heels stepped on toes.

The sun climbed higher and higher.

"Hurry, hurry!" shouted the shoes. "We'll be late! Quick, get inside!"

Most of the shoes climbed inside the first open window they saw and settled under the first bed they could find. Two left men's shoes under Grandma's bed. Wading boots under the bed of two-year-old Caroline. And when my father got up, he found under his bed a lady's pump, a blue sneaker, a left slipper, and a right boy's shoe.

"What in the world . . ." said my father.

"What in the world . . ." said all the people in town when they got out of bed. And that morning a parade of limping people went to work and to school, for they were all wearing the wrong shoes. Either too big or too small. Either two right shoes or two left ones – click-scuff, boom-schwee, schwee-click. Grandma went around in stocking feet, and Caroline went barefoot.

Everyone asked, "Who has my shoes? Who's wearing my shoes?" And everyone examined everyone else's feet. Now and then someone

shouted, "Ah! There's my brown
right shoe!" Or, "Yoo-hoo, you
have my red sandal!" And so,
slowly but surely, everyone got
their own shoes back again.

It took longer for my father,
though, than for anyone else.
Because his left shoe had climbed
a tree, and it was not until three
days later that the wind finally
blew it down.

Baldilocks and the Six Bears

Dick King-Smith

There was once a magic forest full of fine tall trees.

In it lived not only animals, but – because it was a magic forest – fairies and pixies and elves and goblins. Some of the goblins were full of mischief and some of the elves were rather spiteful, but on the whole, the fairy people were a happy lot. All except one.

He was a hobgoblin, quite young, not bad-looking; he might even have been thought handsome except for one thing.

He hadn't a hair on his head.

Someone – probably an elf – had named him Baldilocks, and that was what everyone called him.

Baldilocks had never had a great deal of hair, and what he did have had gradually fallen out, till now he had none at all.

How sad he was. How he envied all the other fairy people their fine locks and tresses, each time they met, at the full moon.

In a clearing among the trees

was a huge fairy-ring, and in the middle of this ring sat the wisest fairy of them all. She was known as the Queen of the Forest.

As usual, everyone laughed when Baldilocks came into the fairy-ring.

"Baldilocks!" someone – probably an elf – would shout, and the pixies would titter and the elves would snigger and the goblins would chuckle and the fairies would giggle. All except one.

She was a little red-haired fairy, not specially beautiful but with such a kindly face. She alone did not laugh at the bald hobgoblin.

116

One night, when everyone was teasing poor Baldilocks as usual, the Queen of the Forest called for silence. Then she said to Baldilocks, "Would you like to grow a fine head of hair?"

"Oh, I would, Your Majesty!" cried the hobgoblin. "But how do I go about it?"

"Ask the bear," said the Queen of the Forest, and not a word more would she say.

The very next morning Baldilocks set out to find a bear. It did not take him long. He came to a muddy pool, and there was a big brown bear, catching frogs.

"Excuse me," said Baldilocks.

"Could you tell me how to grow a fine head of hair?"

The brown bear looked carefully at the hobgoblin. He knew that the only way a bald person can grow hair is by rubbing bear's grease into his scalp. But he wasn't going to say that, because he knew that the only way to get bear's grease is to kill a bear and melt him down.

He picked up a pawful of mud.

"Rub this into your scalp," said the brown bear.

So Baldilocks took the sticky mud and rubbed it on his head. It was full of wriggling things and it smelled horrid. But it didn't make one single hair grow.

The next bear Baldilocks met was a big black one. It was robbing a wild bees' nest.

"Excuse me," said Baldilocks. "Could you tell me how to grow a fine head of hair?"

The black bear looked carefully at the hobgoblin. He too knew the only way for a bald person to grow hair. He pulled out a pawful of honeycomb.

"Rub this into your scalp," said the black bear.

So Baldilocks took the honey and rubbed it on his head. It was horribly sticky and it had several angry bees in it that stung him. But it didn't make one single hair grow.

The third bear that Baldilocks met was a big gingery one, that was digging for grubs in a nettle patch.

Baldilocks asked his question again, and the ginger bear, after looking carefully at him, pulled up a pawful of nettles and said, "Rub these into your scalp."

So Baldilocks took the nettles and rubbed them on his head. They stung him so much that his eyes began to water, but they didn't make one single hair grow.

The fourth bear that Baldilocks came across, a big chocolate-coloured one, was digging out an ant's nest, and by way of reply to the hobgoblin, he handed him a pawful of earth that was full of ants.

When Baldilocks rubbed it on his head, the ants bit him so hard that the tears rolled down his face, but they didn't make one single hair grow.

Baldilocks found the fifth bear by the side of a river that ran through the forest. It was a big old grey bear, and it was eating some fish that had been left high and dry on the bank by a flood. They looked to have been dead for a long time, and when Baldilocks's question had been asked and answered, and he rubbed the rotten fish on his head, they made it smell perfectly awful. But, once again, they didn't make one single hair grow.

Baldilocks had just about had enough. What with the mud and the honey and all the stings and bites and the stink of fish, he almost began to hope that he wouldn't meet another bear. But he did.

It was a baby bear, a little golden one, and it was sitting in the sun doing nothing.

"Excuse me," said Baldilocks. "Could you tell me how to grow a fine head of hair?"

The baby bear looked fearfully at the hobgoblin. He knew, although he was so young, that the only way for a bald person to grow hair is by rubbing bear's grease into his scalp. And he knew, although he was so young, that the only way to get bear's grease is to kill a bear and melt him down.

He did not answer, so Baldilocks, to encourage him, said, "I expect you'll tell me to rub something into my scalp."

"Yes," said the baby bear in a small voice.

"What?"

"Bear's grease," said the baby bear in a small voice.

"Bear's grease?" said Baldilocks. "How do I get hold of that?"

"You have to kill a bear," said the baby bear in a whisper, "and melt him down."

"Oh!" said Baldilocks. "Oh no!" he said.

When next the fairy people met, and the hobgoblin came into the fairy-ring, someone – probably an elf – shouted "Baldilocks!" and everyone laughed, except the little red-haired fairy.

The Queen of the Forest called for silence. Then she said to Baldilocks, "You haven't grown any hair. Didn't you ask a bear?"

"I asked six, Your Majesty," said

Baldilocks, "before I found out that what I need is bear's grease, and to get that I have to kill a bear and melt him down."

"That might be difficult," said the Queen of the Forest, "but perhaps you could kill a little one?"

She smiled as she spoke, because she knew, being the wisest fairy of them all, that high in a nearby tree a small golden bear sat listening anxiously.

"I couldn't do such a thing," said Baldilocks. "I'd sooner stay bald and unhappy."

Up in the tree, the baby bear hugged himself silently.

126

After the others had gone away, Baldilocks still sat alone in the fairy-ring. At least he thought he was alone, till he looked round and saw the little red-haired fairy with the kindly face was still sitting there too.

"I think," she said, "that bald people are much the nicest."

"You do?" said Baldilocks.

"Yes. So you mustn't be unhappy any more. If you are, you will make me very sad."

Baldilocks looked at her, and to his eyes it seemed that she didn't simply have a kind face, she was beautiful.

He smiled the happiest of smiles.

"You mustn't be sad," he said.
"That's something I couldn't
bear."

The Wonderful Cake-Horse

Terry Jones

A man once made a cake shaped like a horse. That night a shooting star flew over the house and a spark happened to fall on the cake-horse. Well, the cake-horse lay there for a few moments. Then it gave a snort. Then it whinnied, scrambled to its legs and shook its mane of white icing, and stood there in the moonlight, gazing round at the world.

The man, who was asleep in bed, heard the noise and looked out of the window, and saw his cake-horse running around the garden, bucking and snorting, just as if it had been a real wild horse.

"Hey! Cake-horse!" cried the man. "What are you doing?"

"Aren't I a fine horse!" cried the cake-horse. "You can ride me if you like."

But the man said, "You've got no horseshoes and you've got no saddle, and you're only made of cake!"

The cake-horse snorted and

bucked and kicked the air, and galloped across the garden, and leaped clean over the gate, and disappeared into the night.

The next morning the cake-horse arrived in the nearby town, and went to the Blacksmith and said, "Blacksmith, make me some good horseshoes, for my feet are only made of cake."

But the blacksmith said, "How will you pay me?"

And the cake-horse answered, "If you make me some horseshoes, I'll be your friend."

But the blacksmith shook his head. "I don't need friends like that!" he said.

So the cake-horse galloped to the saddler, and said, "Saddler! Make me a saddle of the best leather – one that will go with my icing-sugar mane!"

But the saddler said, "If I make you a saddle, how will you pay me?"

"I'll be your friend," said the cake-horse.

"I don't need friends like that!" said the saddler, and shook his head.

The cake-horse snorted and bucked and kicked its legs in the air and said, "Why doesn't anyone want to be my friend? I'll go and join the wild horses!" And he galloped out of the town and off to the moors where the wild horses roamed.

But when he saw the other wild horses, they were all so big and wild that he was afraid they would trample him to crumbs without even noticing he was there.

Just then he came upon a mouse who was groaning to himself under a stone.

"What's the matter with you?" asked the cake-horse.

"Oh," said the mouse, "I ran away from my home in the town, and came up here where there is nothing to eat, and now I'm dying

133

of hunger and too weak to get back."

The cake-horse felt very sorry for the mouse, so it said, "Here you are! You can nibble a bit of me, if you like, for I'm made of cake."

"That's most kind of you," said the mouse, and he ate a little of the cake-horse's tail, and a little of his icing-sugar mane. "Now I feel much better."

Then the cake-horse said, "If only I had a saddle and some horseshoes, I could carry you back to town."

"I'll make you them," said the mouse, and he made four little horseshoes out of acorn cups, and

a saddle out of beetle-shells, and
he got up on the cake-horse's back
and rode him back to town.

And there they remained the
best of friends for the rest of their
lives.

How the Wild Turkey Got Its Spots

Anne Gatti

Long ago, Nganga the wild turkey was black as night. She was a clever bird, always up to tricks, and Lion, the King of the jungle, didn't trust her one bit.

One day Lion was hungry and decided he'd like a good feed of beef. He spotted a cow who had already fought off several other jungle animals with her huge, pointed horns. Lion broke into a run and charged at her. He had just caught up with her and was about to sink his teeth into her shoulders to pull her to the ground when a thick cloud of dust blew up in his face. He coughed and spluttered as the dust choked him. Then he let out a mighty roar as pieces of grit burned his eyes. For several minutes he couldn't see a thing.

When the dust settled he caught sight of Nganga's tail feathers as she scuttled away into the scrub. He realised that the dust cloud must have been her doing.

Lion was furious. Not only had Nganga interrupted his kill, she had also created so much dust that it covered the cow's footprints, and Lion couldn't chase after her. That Nganga was nothing but trouble.

Still, a few days later Lion cheered up when he spied the cow walking down to the stream for a drink. Now he'd get his beef! He crept up on her but the cow must have heard him for she turned just in time and lowered her horns. Lion leaped at her, aiming for her side, when suddenly he was choking all over again, and he fell to the ground, his eyes stinging. This time he could hear Nganga as she puffed and blew, forcing the dust up into a whirling cloud.

When, at last, it settled, the cow had once more disappeared and Nganga was flying off towards the trees.

Lion had had enough. Nganga had spoilt his hunting too many times. He had to get rid of her. He found out where she kept her chicks and lay in wait. After a while she appeared, several chicks running along behind her. He sprang out at her but Nganga was too quick for him and flew up in the air. Then she attacked him from above, pecking his back with her sharp beak. Lion roared and

the chicks screamed and ran for
cover as Nganga kept up her
attack. But it was hard work,
keeping out of reach of his
snarling mouth, and she flew down
to the water for a quick drink.

There on the bank, Nganga saw
the cow with the pointed horns.

"Quick," whispered the cow.

"Over here. Let me help you."

Nganga ran over. The cow, who had wetted the tip of her tail with her milk, swished her tail all over Nganga, sprinkling her with the milk. Then she hid behind a bush. Just then Lion limped up to Nganga who was now a striking, black-and-white spotted bird.

"Have you seen Nganga, by any chance?" he asked.

Nganga disguised her voice and said, "Yes, she went by a few minutes ago. She was heading for the forest."

Lion limped off, in the direction of the forest, and the cow came out of hiding.

141

"What a clever trick!" giggled Nganga. "I couldn't have done better myself. Thank you, my friend, for saving my life – and my chicks."

"A pleasure, dear Nganga. And thank you for saving mine."

Then the cow told Nganga to bring her chicks to be sprinkled with milk too, in case Lion returned.

And that is why the wild turkey has white spots.

Poppy and the Pigeon

Geraldine Kaye

Poppy lives in Small Street.
She lives next door to Tong
and the Singapore Take-Away on
one side and Sam on the other.
There are lots of pigeons in Small
Street. Poppy likes pigeons
because P is for pigeon and for
Poppy too, and pigeons are soft
and grey as a rainy day.

One day at the end of school,
Poppy got her anorak and ran out

to the gate. Mummy wasn't there but Auntie May *was*.

"I'm fetching you today," said Auntie May. "Mummy has gone to hospital to have the new baby."

"Oh," said Poppy surprised. She knew all about the baby coming and Mummy going to hospital of course. And she knew Auntie May was coming to look after her because Daddy was away driving his lorry. But sometimes she forgot because she didn't like Auntie May much.

"Hurry up," said Auntie May as they walked home. "I'm going to spring-clean the whole house this afternoon. Everything has to be clean as a pin for a new baby."

"Can I play with Tong next door?" Poppy said.

"Not today," said Auntie May.

So after tea Poppy went to her bedroom and played with her toys. She thought about Mummy and the new baby and she felt a bit lonely. Downstairs Auntie May tied a duster round her head and got out the vacuum cleaner.

"Clean, clean, clean," sang Auntie May. Zoom, zoom, zoom went the vacuum cleaner.

"Just look at your untidy bedroom," said Auntie May coming upstairs. "How can I clean with toys everywhere?"

So Poppy put her toys in the toy-box and stood by the window. She looked sadly at the garden and the snowdrops which she and Mummy had planted a long time ago. "The baby will come when it's snowdrop time," Mummy had said. They had planted some red-as-a-poppy tulips too but the tulips weren't out yet.

Suddenly Poppy saw something else. A pigeon was sitting on the windowsill on some bits of twig and straw and looking at Poppy with an eye like a yellow bead.

"Just look at your untidy nest!" Poppy said tapping the window and the pigeon flew up startled. In the nest was a small white egg.

"Oh dear, it'll get all cold,"
Poppy said. She knew eggs had to
be kept warm and broke very
easily too. Fortunately the pigeon
flew down again a moment later
and settled back on the nest and
sat there all night.

Next day at breakfast Auntie
May said, "Today I shall clean all

the windows inside and out."

"Oh," said Poppy wondering
what to do. If Auntie May cleaned
the windows outside, she would
surely clean away the pigeon's nest
and the egg as well. After
breakfast Poppy crept upstairs
and opened her bedroom window
very carefully.

"Don't worry, I'll look after your
egg," she whispered as the pigeon
flew up. She wrapped the egg
carefully in Mummy's best hanky
and put it inside the cardboard
egg which Daddy had given her
last Easter. It had been filled with
chocolates then but the chocolates
had gone long ago. The pigeon's

egg fitted snugly inside the cardboard egg and the cardboard egg fitted snugly in the pocket of Poppy's school dress.

"Hurry up," called Auntie May. "I want to phone the hospital."

Poppy put on her anorak very carefully and walked to school very carefully. She was in Mrs Robinson's class.

"I want you all to start with writing today," Mrs Robinson said. Poppy sat at the table with Tong and Sam and Moklissa and they all began writing. But Poppy was thinking about the pigeon's egg in her pocket and she didn't do very good writing.

"Why's your writing gone all squiggly?" Sam said.

"Because . . ." Poppy said but she didn't want to tell anybody about the pigeon's egg. It was a secret. When the buzzer went for playtime, everybody ran out except Poppy.

"Aren't you going out to play?" said Mrs Robinson.

"I . . . I think I'll just sit still," Poppy said.

"Aren't you feeling well?" said Mrs Robinson putting her hand on Poppy's forehead. "Do you want to lie down?"

"Yes, please," Poppy said and she lay down on the special for-people-who-aren't-feeling-well sofa and stayed there until dinner time.

"I think Poppy's missing her mummy," Mrs Robinson said when Auntie May came to fetch her. "Any news of the baby yet?"

"A little boy," said Auntie May. "Born early this morning. I've just come from the hospital."

"First baby this year in Small Street," Mrs Robinson said.

"He's going to be called *James*," Poppy said. "Can I go and see him right now? Oh please . . ."

"Not today," said Auntie May. "Mummy's resting. Perhaps tomorrow."

After tea Poppy went up to her

151

bedroom. The windowsill was scrubbed clean and the nest had gone. But the pigeon was sitting on the roof of Sam's house next door.

"I'll make you a new nest right now," Poppy whispered and she ran to Daddy's sock drawer and found some yellow and brown socks the same colour as the twigs and straw. She made a nest of socks for the pigeon's egg and the pigeon flew down and settled on the sock nest on the windowsill.

That night Poppy got into bed and went straight to sleep. When she woke in the morning, Daddy was home.

"Do you want to come and fetch Mummy and James?" he said.

"Oh yes . . . oh yes . . ." said Poppy jumping up and down.

Baby James had pink wrinkly skin with a wisp of dark hair. Poppy quite liked him though he did cry rather a lot.

After that Auntie May went away and Daddy stayed at home all the time and the pigeon went on sitting on the sock nest. A few days later the egg hatched into a baby pigeon.

"Second baby in Small Street," Poppy whispered. It had pink wrinkled skin too at first but soon its feathers grew, white and then soft and grey as a rainy day. By the time the red tulips came out it was big enough to fly away and baby James had smiled his first smile.

Poppy never told anybody about the pigeon or the egg but one hot summer night Daddy opened the bedroom window wide.

"How did my best brown and yellow socks get out here?" he said. Poppy didn't say anything and Daddy never did find out.

But you know how they got there, don't you?

Lucy's Wish

Adèle Geras

Every day Lucy asked, "What's the date?" hoping that the answer would be "Christmas Day".

One day, she asked her question in the supermarket as her mother was pushing her round in the trolley.

"It's only October 23rd," said Lucy's mother, "but we're making the Christmas cake today."

Lucy smiled. She loved getting

ready for Christmas.

At home, Lucy helped her mother prepare everything she needed to make the cake. Apart from the flour and eggs and sugar and margarine, there were all the packets they had brought in the supermarket: raisins, currants, sultanas, cherries, mixed peel and flaked almonds. Lucy put some of them into the bowl, and at the end she had to stir the squelchy beige mixture that was full of unexpected bits and lumps. As she stirred, she had to make a special wish.

"What did you wish for?" Mum asked Lucy.

"I'm not telling," said Lucy. "The wish doesn't work if you tell anyone what it is."

After the cake had been made, days and days went by and nothing at all was said about Christmas. Then . . .

"What's the date?" asked Lucy.

"November 30th," said her sister Frances, who was eight. "I think we ought to start making the decorations."

"Yes, let's," said Lucy.

So Lucy and Frances sat in the kitchen with a big pot of paste and lots of red and green paper and made snakes of paper chains to go all round the walls. Frances made a big holly wreath and let Lucy stick the satin bow on it.

All afternoon the girls sat at the big table by the window as the houses across the road grew darker and darker, until they looked like black paper cut-outs against the sky that turned pink as the sun went down, then mauve, then blue.

"Look," said Frances. "There's the first star. Make a wish, quickly."

Lucy closed her eyes and wished.

"What did you wish?" asked Frances.

"I'm not telling," said Lucy. "The wish doesn't work if you tell anyone what it is."

After the decorations had been made, counting the days became easier. Lucy and Frances each had an advent calendar, and every day, they each opened a small door and looked at the picture inside.

On December 15th, Lucy's dad said, "I've got the Christmas tree in the garage, girls. Time to go and fetch all that stuff from the attic to put on it."

So up into the attic went Lucy and Frances and their dad, and found the boxes full of what Lucy called the Tree Jewels.

They brought the boxes downstairs and hung thin balls

of shiny silver and purple and midnight blue from the branches. They looped golden tinsel around the tree, tied red ribbons into bows with long, trailing ends, and balanced small silver-paper covered stars and moon shapes among the dark pine needles.

"Lucy," said Dad, "come and I'll hold you up while you put the Fairy Queen on top here. Don't forget to make a wish, now." Lucy closed her eyes and wished.

"What did you wish for?" asked Dad.

"I'm not telling," said Lucy. "The wish doesn't work if you tell anyone what it is."

On Christmas Eve, Lucy couldn't sleep.

"Why can't you sleep?" asked Frances.

"I'm sad," said Lucy.

"How can you be sad on Christmas Eve?"

"I'm sad because my wish didn't come true. Even though I wished for it three times."

"What did you wish?"

"It was silly. I don't want to say." Lucy turned her face into the pillow.

"Well, go to sleep then. It's Christmas Day tomorrow."

Lucy thought about her wish. Perhaps it really had been silly to

163

hope that the garden, which was full of fallen leaves and bare bark trees and dark earth could be pretty again. Lucy knew that leaves and flowers came in the spring, but it seemed unfair to her that when everything *inside* was so warm and beautiful the garden should be so cold and empty. She looked out of her window.

"Maybe," she thought, "I'll try again. Just once more." Lucy closed her eyes and wished. Then she lay down and fell asleep.

In the morning, Frances woke up first.

"Lucy," she whispered. "It's time to wake up. Let's see what's in our stockings."

Lucy woke up and together the girls ate the satsumas and nuts and raisins that someone had put into their Christmas stockings during the night.

"It's very sunny," said Frances. "You can tell even though the curtains are closed."

"Let's open them," said Lucy. "You pull that one and I'll pull this one."

The curtains opened.

"Look!" whispered Lucy. "Oh Frances, look! My wish came true in the night."

The garden glittered in the sun. Every branch and twig and blade of grass, every roof and windowsill, the dark brown earth and the green tops of hedges, everything was thick with snow. The window of Lucy and Frances's bedroom had frost all around the edges of the glass, like a border of white flowers.

"How lovely it looks!" said Lucy. "I never thought it would look as pretty as that."

"Is that what you wished for?" asked Frances. "Did you wish for snow?"

"I didn't know I wished for it," said Lucy, "but I suppose I must have done."

"What did you say, then?"

166

"I just closed my eyes and said, 'I wish the garden could be decorated for Christmas.'"

"Well," said Frances, "it *is* decorated. Well done. You must wish again next year."

"I will," said Lucy. "Is it time for presents yet?"

The girls crept into their mum and dad's room.

"Wake up!" said Lucy. "It's Christmas Day, and my wish came true!"

Teddy Robinson Goes to the Dolls' Hospital

Joan G. Robinson

One day Teddy Robinson was waving goodbye to Daddy when he waved so hard that all of a sudden his arm came right off.

"Oh, my goodness," he said, very surprised to see his arm in Deborah's hand without the rest of him joined on to it, "I seem to be going all to pieces."

168

"Never mind, my poor boy," said Deborah, "Mummy will mend it."

But Mummy said she could only sew it on, and then it wouldn't be able to swivel round any more.

"And what's the good of that?" said Teddy Robinson. "I *must* have an arm that swivels round." And he was so set on it that Mummy said he had better go to the Dolls' Hospital.

So off they went to the toy shop, which was also the Dolls' Hospital. Teddy Robinson was so pleased to be going that he sang all the way there, and Deborah hardly had a chance to remind him about saying please and thank

you, and not showing off, and not
singing too loudly in the middle of
the night.

The man in the Dolls' Hospital
said yes, he could mend Teddy
Robinson's arm and they could
fetch him again on Friday.

"This is his nightie," said
Deborah, handing a little bag over
the counter, "and when are
visiting days, please?"

"Oh dear," said the man, "I don't
usually have visiting days. People
just come when it's time to fetch
them again."

Deborah was rather
disappointed. She had hoped she
would be able to see all the dolls in

170

their little cots and beds.

"It doesn't seem fair," she said.
"He came with me when I went to
hospital."

But the man promised to take
good care of him, and as he looked
the sort of man who understood
teddy bears, Deborah decided not
to mind and kissed Teddy
Robinson goodbye.

After that he was taken into a
room behind the shop where all
the other animals and dolls were
waiting to be mended. The man
put him up on the top shelf next to
a stuffed horse and a felt cat; then
he went back to the shop.

The stuffed horse looked at

Teddy Robinson. He lowered his
head; his legs slipped out
sideways.

"Horsey's the name," he said.
"How do you do? No need to ask
why you're here – I see you've lost
an arm, poor fellow."

"Oh no, I haven't lost it," said
Teddy Robinson. "I've brought it

with me. It just needs fixing on again."

"My trouble's of long standing," said the horse. "You see, it's my legs. They slide out sideways and then I fall on my nose. I'm hoping to get new wires put in them."

The felt cat stared hard at Teddy Robinson as if she wanted to be noticed. He smiled politely.

"I hope you are not here for anything serious?" he asked.

"It's my insides," said the cat, smiling proudly. "My squeak is worn out. They're going to put a new one in, *if* they can, which I very much doubt." She purred softly. "I'm not at all an easy case."

"Oh, I'm sorry," said Teddy Robinson.

"*I* don't mind," said the cat. "It's very interesting. Makes something to talk about. I like coming here."

"Have you been here before, then?"

"Oh, yes, often. There's nothing I haven't had done – new ears, new eyes, re-stuffing, everything."

"Fancy that," said Teddy Robinson, "and I thought I was quite important coming only once."

The dolls all made quite a fuss of Teddy Robinson because he was the only teddy bear there. They

174

called him Teddy right from the start, so he decided not to bother about his second name as he didn't want to make himself seem more special than anyone else.

And then the Other Bear arrived. He was a new-looking bear with golden-yellow fur, and when he was brought in all the dolls said, "Oooh, what a handsome teddy bear! Shall we call him Goldie?"

But the Other Bear said, "No thank you. I prefer to be called by my own name. It is rather a distinguished one." He then bowed slightly from the waist, looking very proud and handsome, and

said, "You may call me Teddy
Robinson."

"Hi!" called Teddy Robinson
from the top shelf, "you can't do
that. It's my name."

"Oh, no," said the felt cat, "you
can't have it too. He thought of it
first – a most distinguished name."

"You can have Brown for a
second name," said one of the dolls
kindly. "It will suit you."

So from then on Teddy Robinson
was called Teddy Brown, and the
Other Bear was called Teddy
Robinson, which made the real
Teddy Robinson very cross indeed.

The dolls made as much fuss of
the Other Bear as they had made

of Teddy Robinson. He told them he was there because one of his legs was loose, although he was still almost new.

"I was expensive," he said, "so it should never have happened. I think it's because I've been shown off so much. I'm rather a special bear, you see. I'm told some one has even written a book about me."

"You *are* lucky to be such a Special bear," said the dolls.

"Oh, yes," said the Other Bear, "but I suppose we can't all be Special, and I expect even quite ordinary bears with names like Smith or Brown have people who are quite fond of them."

Just then the shop man came in, carrying a beautiful big doll. She was wearing a pink silk dress with a bonnet to match and she had a very pretty face. But her eyes were closed.

Teddy Robinson looked over the top shelf and saw that it was Jacqueline. Jacqueline was a doll he knew. She belonged to a little girl called Mary Anne who was a friend of Deborah. Teddy Robinson had always admired Jacqueline ever since she had come to his birthday party and laughed at all his jokes. Her eyes had been shut even then, but she had never stopped smiling all through the party.

The shop man laid Jacqueline down gently on the bottom shelf, next to the Other Bear, then he went out again.

"Oooh!" said all the dolls. "A Sleeping Beauty!"

Jacqueline smiled sweetly, then said, "Tell me, is my friend Teddy Robinson still in the hospital?"

"Why, yes!" they said, "he is right beside you."

Up on the top shelf the real Teddy Robinson was doing his best to fall at Jacqueline's feet and tell her that *he* was the real one.

"Stop pushing," said the horse.

"You'll only upset everybody. We don't all want to fall off the shelf."

"But I know her!" said Teddy Robinson.

"Why all the fuss?" said the felt cat. "Can't somebody ask her if she knows Teddy Brown?"

"Teddy Brown?" said Jacqueline, "no, I've never heard of him."

"There you are, you see," said the felt cat, "she doesn't know you at all. It's Teddy Robinson she knows, and I'm not surprised – such a distinguished name. Now do sit quiet."

So poor Teddy Robinson had to sit tight while the others talked down below.

180

"I've come to have my eyes
unstuck," he heard Jacqueline say.
"They were shut even when I came
to your party, do you remember?"

"No, I can't say I do," said the
Other Bear, who, of course, hadn't
been at Teddy Robinson's party at
all.

"Who is that growling up there?"
asked Jacqueline suddenly.

"Teddy Brown," said the dolls.
"Take no notice."

"What a bad-tempered bear,"
said Jacqueline. Then she said to
the Other Bear, smiling sweetly,
"Don't you really remember me,
Teddy Robinson?"

"No, I'm afraid not," said the

Other Bear, "but of course I meet so many pretty dolls I could hardly remember them all."

"I never thought Teddy Robinson would forget me," said Jacqueline sadly. "I always remember him and how beautifully he sang."

"Yes," said the Other Bear, "I am told I have quite a good voice – a sort of bearitone," and he began making a sort of growling la-la-la noise.

"Are you *sure* you're Teddy Robinson?" said Jacqueline, looking puzzled. "You sound so different."

"Of course I'm sure," said the

Other Bear.

"And yet," said Jacqueline, "Teddy Robinson used to make up proper songs, with his own words, not just la-la-la."

"All right, so can I," said the Other Bear, and after a lot of coughing and humming and ha-ing he sang:

*"I – er – ah – um, here's a song
all about er – um – ah – um,
hear me sing – er – sing a song,
la-la-la-la tumty-tum."*

"No," said Jacqueline, "you're not Teddy Robinson at all. I didn't think you could be. Teddy Robinson is not only the handsomest and cleverest bear I know. He is also the most modest. And he would never call *that* singing."

Up on the top shelf the real Teddy Robinson was thinking round and round in his head. He had been quite sure he was Teddy Robinson until he heard Jacqueline say what a bad-tempered bear he was. Then he began to wonder.

"How can I be sure I'm me?" he asked the horse quietly.

"Who else do you feel like?" said the horse in a horse whisper.

"Well, I'm not feeling quite

184

myself," said Teddy Robinson, "but I thought it was having only one arm." He began singing softly:

> *"Am I me?*
> *Or am I me?*
> *And if I'm not,*
> *Who can I be?"*

"I know that voice!" cried Jacqueline, down below.

"It's the silly bear on the top shelf," said the dolls.

"Do let him go on," said Jacqueline, and when Teddy Robinson heard this he knew that of course he was himself, even if he didn't *feel* quite himself, and he sang out at the top of his voice:

"Stick me up
or blow me down,
call me Smith
or call me Brown
call me Jones
for all I care,
call me just a silly bear,
But I'm still Teddy Robinson and
nobody else, so there!"

And then, because he had no breath left, he overbalanced, and with a cry of "Jacqueline!" he fell at her feet with a bump.

"Oh, my dear Teddy Robinson, is it really you?" she said. "I'm so glad! Who ever is this silly Other Bear who's been calling

186

himself you?"

All the others began talking at once, saying, "Fancy that", "The Other Bear took his name", "What a shame!" but Teddy Robinson and Jacqueline hardly heard them, they had so much to say to each other.

As for the Other Bear, he never said a word, but just sat straight and proud, pretending not to notice, until the shop man came in and fetched him away to be mended.

After that it was Teddy Robinson's turn. When his arm had been fixed on again the man pinned a label on him and carried him into the shop. There on the counter sat the Other Bear, also with a label on, all ready to go home.

The man put them down side by side, but the two teddy bears took no notice of each other. Each of them was trying hard to read the other one's label without looking. Then all of a sudden they both looked very surprised indeed.

"I say!" said Teddy Robinson, "is that your label?"

"Yes," said the Other Bear. "Is that yours?" For both the labels had Teddy Robinson written on them.

"I say, I'm awfully sorry," said

Teddy Robinson. "I'd no idea there was anyone else in the world with the same name as me. You must have had rather a horrid time in there with everyone thinking you were pretending to be me. No wonder you were so quiet."

"Least said soonest mended," said the Other Bear, "and I *was* soonest mended."

"So you were," said Teddy Robinson. "But I am sorry."

"I thought you were making it up," said the Other Bear. "After all, Robinson is such a distinguished name. I'm surprised at *you* having it."

They were still both busy being

surprised when the shop man came back, carrying a big telephone book.

"They asked me to phone when this one was ready," he said to his wife, "and now I've gone and lost their number." He turned over the pages. "Hmmm," he said, "just as I thought, pages and pages of Robinsons. Why, there must be more than a thousand of them. I'll never find the right one."

He went away again, scratching his head.

"Pages and pages of Robinsons?" said Teddy Robinson. "Well, bless my braces!"

"*And*," said the Other Bear

190

solemnly, "if even half of those Robinsons have teddy bears it means there must be about four-hundred-and-ninety-nine other Teddy Robinsons, besides me."

"What about me?" said Teddy Robinson.

"You're just one of the four-hundred-and-ninety-nine other ones," said the Other Bear.

"Well, blow me up and stick me down, I think I'll change my name to Brown," said Teddy Robinson.

But at that minute the shop door opened and in came Deborah and Mummy. Teddy Robinson forgot all about changing his name to Brown, and all about all the other

Teddy Robinsons, he was so pleased to see them.

Deborah hugged him and admired his mended arm.

"How does it feel to have two again?" she asked.

"Fine," said Teddy Robinson, swivelling it round as fast as it would go. "I got so used to having only one that it felt like having two, so now I've got two it feels more like three. I only need one more and I shall feel like a windmill."

Just then Deborah saw the Other Bear on the counter.

"*Look*, Mummy!" she said. "It's another Teddy Robinson."

192

"Why, so it is!" said Mummy.

"How funny that such an ordinary-looking bear should have our name," said Deborah.

"Well, ours is a very ordinary name," said Mummy, laughing. "There must be hundreds of Teddy Robinsons, when you come to think of it."

"But only one really Special one like mine," said Deborah, hugging him all over again.

And that is the end of the story about how Teddy Robinson went to the Dolls' Hospital.

ACKNOWLEDGEMENTS

The publishers wish to thank the following for permission to reproduce copyright material:

Paul Biegel: for "The Naughty Shoes", translated by Celia Amidon, included in *A Pocketful of Stories for Five-Year Olds*, ed. Pat Thomson, published by Doubleday 1991, reproduced by permission of the author.

Annette Elizabeth Clark: for "The Tale of Mrs Puffin's Prize Pumpkin" from *Country Tales* by Annette Elizabeth Clark, first published by Hodder and Stoughton Children's Books, reproduced by permission of Hodder & Stoughton Ltd.

Berlie Doherty: for "Wonderful Worms" from *Tilly Mint Tales* by Berlie Doherty, first published by Methuen Children's Books 1984, reproduced by permission of David Higham Associates on behalf of the author.

Dorothy Edwards: for "My Naughty Little Sister and the Big Girl's Bed" from *More Naughty Little Sister Stories* by Dorothy Edwards, first published by Methuen Children's Books 1989. Copyright © 1989 Dorothy Edwards, reproduced by permission of Rogers, Coleridge & White Ltd on behalf of the author.

Anne Gatti: for "How the Wild Turkey Got Its Spots" from *Tales from the African Plains* by Anne Gatti, this edition published by Pavilion 1997, reproduced by permission of Pavilion Books.

Adèle Geras: for "Lucy's Wish" from *Stories for Bedtime* by Adèle Geras, first published by Collins Children's Books 1995. Copyright © Adèle Geras 1995, reproduced by permission of Laura Cecil Literary Agency on behalf of the author.

Anita Hewitt: for "A Hat for Rhinoceros" from *The Anita Hewitt Animal Story Book*, first published by Bodley Head 1972, reproduced by permission of The Random House Group Ltd.

Terry Jones: for "The Wonderful Cake-Horse" from *Fairy Tales* by Terry Jones, first published by Pavilion 1981, reproduced by permission of Pavilion Books.

Geraldine Kaye: for "Poppy and the Pigeon" from *Birthdays in Small Street* by Geraldine Kaye, first published by Methuen Children's Books 1993. Copyright © 1993 Geraldine Kaye, reproduced by permission of Egmont Children's Books Ltd.

ACKNOWLEDGEMENTS

Dick King-Smith: for "Baldilocks and the Six Bears" from *The Ghost at Codlin Castle and Other Stories* by Dick King-Smith, first published by Viking 1992, reproduced by permission of A P Watt Ltd on behalf of Fox Busters Ltd.

Margaret Mahy: for "The Rare Spotted Birthday Party" from *Leaf Magic* by Margaret Mahy, first published by J M Dent, reproduced by permission from The Orion Publishing Group Ltd.

Andrew Matthews: for "Lazy Jack" from *Silly Stories* by Andrew Matthews, first published by Orion Children's Books 1995, reproduced by permission from The Orion Publishing Group Ltd.

Joan G. Robinson: for "Teddy Robinson Goes to the Dolls' Hospital" from *Dear Teddy Robinson* by Joan G. Robinson, first published by Puffin 1966. Copyright © J. G. Robinson 1956/1960, reproduced by permission from Penguin Books Ltd.

Every effort has been made to trace the copyright holders but where this has not been possible or where any error has been made the publishers will be pleased to make the necessary arrangement at the first opportunity.

Animal stories

for 5 year olds

Chosen by Helen Paiba

A bright and varied selection of
heart-warming animal stories by some
of the very best writers for children.
Perfect for reading alone or aloud — and for
dipping into time and time again.
With stories from Dick King-Smith,
Joyce Lankester Brisley, Dorothy Edwards,
Margaret Mahy and many more, this book
will provide hours of fantastic fun.

Funny stories

for 5 Year Olds

Chosen by Helen Paiba

A bright and varied selection of wonderfully
entertaining stories by some of the very
best writers for children. Perfect for
reading alone or aloud – and for dipping into
time and time again. With stories from
Dick King-Smith, Tony Ross, Alf Prøysen,
Malorie Blackman and many more,
this book will provide hours of fantastic fun.

Magical stories

for 5 year olds

Chosen by Helen Paiba

A bright and varied selection of
marvellously magical stories
by some of the very best writers
for children. Perfect for reading alone or
aloud – and for dipping into time
and time again. With stories from
Joan Aiken, Margaret Mayo,
Alf Prøysen, Margaret Mahy and
many more, this book will
provide hours of fantastic fun.